Mr. Belinsky's Bagels

For Gussie and Joe
–E. S.

For Marcia
–S. C.

Paperback edition first published in 1999
Second Printing 2005
by Tradewind Books Limited
202-1807 Maritime Mews, Granville Island, Vancouver, BC V6H3W7
email: tradewindbooks@yahoo.com
www.tradewindbooks.com

Marilyn Bagel is the author of *The Bagel Bible: For Bagel Lovers,*
The Complete Guide to Great Noshing (The Globe Pequot Press, 1992)

Designed by Andrew Johnstone
Hand-lettering by Susan King
Assistant to illustrator Michael Haijtink

Printed and bound in China
10 9 8 7 6 5 4 3

Cataloguing-in-Publication Data
for this book is available from
The British Library

Canadian Cataloguing in Publication Data

Schwartz, Ellen, 1949-
Mr. Belinsky's bagels

ISBN 1-896580-14-9 (bound)
ISBN 1-896580-28-9 (paperback)

I. Czernecki, Stefan, 1946-   II. Title
PS8587.C578M57 1997   jC813'.54   C97-910314-2

Mr. Belinsky's Bagels

Ellen Schwartz

Illustrated by Stefan Czernecki

LONDON AND VANCOUVER

Mr. Belinsky made bagels. Bagels were all he made. He didn't make pies, he didn't make cakes, he didn't make doughnuts or muffins or gingerbread. He just made bagels—poppy seed, onion, and pumpernickel bagels—and he sold them in his shop, called BELINSKY'S BAGELS.

Mr. Belinsky's son, Victor, said, "Pa, why do you make only bagels? Why don't you make cinnamon rolls or butter rolls or jelly rolls?"

Mr. Belinsky answered, "Should a doctor fix leaky pipes? No! Should an opera singer take care of sick dogs? No! Should Belinsky make fancy cakes? NO! I make bagels. Bagels is what I make. And that's that."

Such bagels! So delicious! Yet Mr. Belinsky had no recipe. He simply threw water, yeast, flour, and salt in a bowl. As he kneaded, his fingers felt the secrets of the dough.

"The recipe," he said, "is in my hands."

Every day Mrs. Alperstein came in for a poppy seed bagel. Every day she had a new ailment.

"Oh, Mr. Belinsky, my hip! How it aches! And the noise it makes–cr-r-rick, cr-r-rick–like a broken-down train!"

"There, there, Mrs. Alperstein, a fresh poppy seed bagel will make you feel better," Mr. Belinsky would say.

Sure enough, no sooner had Mrs. Alperstein taken a bite than her pain went away. "Mr. Belinsky, I feel better already! I'm telling you, it's the poppy seeds."

Frankie went for the onion bagels. Frankie was tough. He stomped. He swaggered. He scowled. Everybody was scared of Frankie.

Everybody but Mr. Belinsky. He just laughed. "You don't fool me, Frankie. I see you help old people across the street. I see you coo at babies. Tough guy, ha!"

Frankie blushed. Then he growled, "Don't tell anybody–or else!"

Mr. Belinsky winked.

Josh loved the pumpernickel bagels. He was Mr. Belinsky's helper. Mr. Belinsky kept a small apron on a hook for him. Every day Josh came in and twisted the pumpernickel dough into little brown circles. He always ate the first pumpernickel bagel out of the oven—just to make sure the batch was good.

"Josh," Mr. Belinsky said, "you are the best helper a bagel baker ever had."

Mr. Belinsky was happy. So his little shop was old and cramped. Who cared? His customers loved his bagels, and that was that.

Across the street from Belinsky's Bagels there was an empty store. One day workers arrived with ladders and hammers, wood and paint. Brown paper covered the windows. From inside came pounding and sawing and banging.

Mr. Belinsky wondered what kind of store it would be. A pet shop? A toy store? A dress shop?

After many days, the brown paper came down. An enormous sign lit up:
BON BON BAKERY

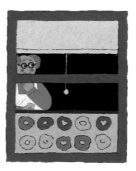

All day Mr. Belinsky watched as people bypassed his store and streamed into the Bon Bon Bakery.

That evening Victor came by. "See, Pa?" he said, pointing at the new shop. "You've got to make pies, cakes, and cookies. Not just bagels."

Mr. Belinsky shook his head. "I make bagels. Bagels is what I make."

"Come, Pa," Victor said, and he led his father across the street. Mr. Belinsky peeked in. Eager customers were buying delectable pastries.

Mr. Belinsky turned. His own store was empty.

"Victor is right," he thought with alarm. "I must do something."

The next day, Mr. Belinsky made chocolate chip cookies. People crowded into the shop. "Delicious!" they said. "Scrumptious!" they shouted. And they bought all the cookies.

Mrs. Alperstein came in. "Mr. Belinsky, my elbow, how it aches! Give me a poppy seed bagel, quick!"

"Mrs. Alperstein . . . you see . . . too busy . . . I have no poppy seed bagels today."

"Excuse me, Mr. Belinsky? I didn't hear so good. I thought you said there were no poppy seed bagels."

Mr. Belinsky hung his head.

Mrs. Alperstein left, moaning.

Mr. Belinsky felt terrible. But what a success the cookies were!

Soon Mr. Belinsky was baking oatmeal cookies and blackberry tarts, pecan pies and apple strudel. His happy customers bought everything. Mr. Belinsky was proud. Belinsky's Bagels had never been so popular. Popular and crowded and noisy and busy...

Frankie came in. The onion bagel bin was full of eclairs.

"Mr. B, what's with the gooey stuff? Where are the onion bagels?"

"Sorry, Frankie, no time."

"No onion bagels?"

"No onion bagels."

A tear spilled down Frankie's cheek. Quickly he wiped it away. Then he stomped out.

"Oh, dear," Mr. Belinsky said.

Next Mr. Belinsky bought machines. Egg beaters and pastry puffers and cake decorators whipped and puffed and whirred. Meringues and muffins and macaroons spilled out of the ovens.

"Look how much money I'm making!" Mr. Belinsky said.

But every night, when he counted the money, his hands felt...as though they were missing something. But he couldn't remember what.

One day Josh came in. He put on his apron. But there was no pumpernickel dough. Mr. Belinsky was frosting a grand chocolate cake.

"Mr. Belinsky, no pumpernickel bagels?"

Mr. Belinsky's face turned red. "No pumpernickel."

"Onion?" Josh said.

"No onion."

"Poppy seed?"

"No poppy seed."

"NO BAGELS?"

There was a pause. "No bagels."

"But Mr. Belinsky," Josh said, "you make bagels!"

The entire store fell silent. Josh threw down his apron and ran out the door.

Mr. Belinsky stood there, red-faced. Then he said, "Belinsky's Bagels is closed."

Mr. Belinsky chased all the customers out the door. He tossed out the new machines. Then he took out his old mixing bowl.

"Was it this much water?" he asked himself. "How much yeast? What kind of flour?"

"I've forgotten," he thought with alarm. "Forgotten how to make bagels!"

He paced. He scratched his head. Nothing.

His eyes filled with tears.

Absentmindedly, he let warm water run into the bowl...sprinkled yeast on the water...dumped in some flour...and started kneading.

"What a fool I've been," he thought, "and now I've..."

"Remembered! My hands remembered!"

Just then, Victor came in. "Pa, what's going on?" Grinning, Mr. Belinsky held out his hands. "Victor, you see these hands? They are wise. Wiser than my foolish, mixed-up head."

"What? Pa, where are all the goodies? Where are all the machines?"

"Gone, and good riddance," Mr. Belinsky said with a wave of his hand.

"WHAT!" Victor said. "Pa, forgive me, but you must have a hole in your head! What about your new customers?"

"Victor," Mr. Belinsky said, "I make bagels. Bagels is what I make."

And he laughed.

The next morning, Mr. Belinsky welcomed his three loyal customers into Belinsky's Bagels.

"A poppy seed bagel for Mrs. Alperstein, to cure all aches and pains. An onion bagel for my favourite kind-hearted tough guy. And a pumpernickel bagel for the very best bagel baker's helper."

Just then Victor arrived.

"Victor!" Mr. Belinsky cried. "Come in, come in! Have a bagel!"

Victor grinned. He hugged his father. "Don't mind if I do, Pa." And he bit into a fresh bagel.

Mr. Belinsky grinned, too. "I make bagels. Bagels is what I make. And that's that!"

Who made the first bagel?

No one knows for sure, but it is said that in 1683 in Vienna, Austria, a Jewish baker wanted to thank the king of Poland for protecting the country against attack from an invading army.

The baker knew the king's favourite hobby was horseback riding. "I've got it!" he thought. "I'll make him special hard rolls in the shape of a riding stirrup!" *Bügel* is the word for "stirrup" in German.

Bagels have come a long way since then. They first arrived in America more than ninety years ago. In Montreal and New York City, they were sold from pushcarts on the cobblestone streets. Today, billions of bagels are eaten by everyone from teething infants to their great-grandparents.

—*Marilyn Bagel*

Marilyn Bagel is the author of *The Bagel Bible*.